Mel Bay Presents

AMERICAN LOVE SONGS & BALLADS

By Jerry Silverman

Contents

Foreword

From "Roses are red, violets are blue, sugar is sweet, and so are you," to a four-act grand opera, the love song is the most common form of human musical expression. The songs in this collection fall somewhere in-between those two extremes—more like young men carving hearts and arrows on the old oak tree, and young women confiding in their diaries.

The Anglo-American love song sings equally of "true lovers" and "false true lovers." Happiness goes hand in hand with heartbreak; hope with hopelessness.

The cast of characters includes: Both "fair and tender girls," and "fair and tender ladies" (a nice distinction), headstrong daughters and hopeful suitors, the forsaken and the forsakers, the betrayers and the betrayed, and oh, yes—happy couples!

A deceptively simple pentatonic southern ballad, like *At the Foot of Yonder Mountain,* can hold its own lyrically and musically with a jazzy, chromatic Tin Pan Alley number, like *My Melancholy Baby.* On opposite ends of the musical spectrum, they both express the same emotions of longing and desire. The reader may find it at first a little unusual to encounter such a wide divergence of musical styles in one song book. However, on closer inspection, except for an occasional "extra" sharp or flat, or chord progression, they are not so different after all.

Folksingers should enjoy the more complex sounds of well-crafted "composed" songs. (Well, all songs were composed. It's just that we don't always know who dunnit.) Singers of "popular" songs should equally enjoy becoming acquainted with their musical roots. Smack in the middle of these two camps are the songs of Stephen Collins Foster, bridging the gap between the earlier anonymous tradition and the artfully crafted composition. "All the world loves a lover" —so the saying goes. I would amend that by adding, "All the world loves a love song."

Jerry Silverman

Come All You Fair and Tender Girls

Come all you fair and ten - der girls That flour- ish in your

prime, ___ prime, Be - ware, be - ware, make your gar - den ___ fair. Let

no man steal ___ your thyme, ___ thyme, Let ___ no man ___ steal ___ your ___ thyme.

And when your thyme is past and gone
He'll care no more for you.
And every day that your garden is waste
Will spread all over with rue, rue.
Will spread all over with rue.

A woman is a branched tree
And man a singing wind.
And from her branches carelessly
He'll take what he can find, find.
He'll take what he can find.

A Railroader For Me

Now I would not marry a blacksmith,
He's always in the black,
I'd rather marry an engineer
That throws the throttle back. *Chorus*

I would not marry a farmer,
He's always in the dirt,
I'd rather marry an engineer
That wears a striped shirt. *Chorus*

I would not marry a cowboy,
A-ridin' the western plain,
I'd rather marry an engineer
Who wears a big watch-chain. *Chorus*

I would not marry a sheriff,
For he is sure to die,
But I would marry a railroader
Who has them pretty blue eyes. *Chorus*

I would not marry a preacher,
He preaches too much hell,
But I would marry a railroader
Who rings the engine bell. *Chorus*

I would not marry a gambler
Who's always drinkin' wine,
But I would marry a railroader
Who drives the forty-nine. *Chorus*

Father, oh dear father,
Forgive me if you can,
If you ever see your daughter again
It's be with a railroad man. *Chorus*

At The Foot Of Yonder Mountain

- Canon -

At the foot of yon - der moun - tain there runs a clear stream, At the

foot of yon - der moun - tain there lives a fair queen. She's

hand - some, she's prop - er, And her ways__ are com - plete. I_____

ask no oth - er pas - time than to be with my sweet.

But why she won't have me I well understand:
She wants some freeholder and I have no land.
I cannot maintain her on silver and gold,
And all the other fine things that my love's house should hold.

Oh, I wish I were a penman and could write a fine hand!
I would write my love a letter from this distant land.
I'd send it by the waters just for to let her know
That I think of pretty Mary wherever I go.

Oh, I wish I were a bird and had wings and could fly.
It's to my love's window this night I'd draw nigh.
I'd sit in her window all night long and cry
That for love of pretty Mary I gladly would die.

Come All Ye Fair And Tender Ladies

They'll tell to you some loving story,
They'll declare to you their love is true;
Straightway they'll go and court some other,
And that's the love they have for you.

I wish I was some little sparrow,
That I had wings and I could fly;
I'd fly away to my false true lover,
And when he's talking I'd be nigh.

But I am not a little sparrow,
And neither have I wings to fly;
I'll sit down here in grief and sorrow
To weep and pass my troubles by.

If I'd a-known before I courted,
I never would have courted none;
I'd have locked my heart in a box of golden,
And pinned it up with a silver pin.

Don't Sing Love Songs

like a 5-string banjo

" All men are false," says my mother,
" They'll tell you wicked, lovely lies,
And the very next evening, court another
Leaving you alone to pine and sigh."

My father is a handsome devil,
He's got a chain that's five miles long,
And every link a heart does dangle
Of some poor maid he's loved and wronged.

Wish that I was some little sparrow,
Yes, one of those that flies so high,
I'd fly away to my false true lover,
And when he'd speak I would deny.

On his breast, I'd light and flutter
With my little tender wings,
I'd ask him who he meant to flatter,
Or who he meant to deceive.

Go court some other tender lady,
And I hope that she will be your wife,
'Cause I've been warned and I've decided
To sleep alone all my life.

He's Gone Away

I'm goin' a - way _ for to stay a lit - tle while. But I'm com-ing back, if I go the thou - sand miles. Oh, who will tie your shoes? And who will glove your hand? And who will kiss those ru - by lips when I am gone? Look a - way, look a - way o - ver Yan - dro.

He's gone away for to stay a little while,
But he's coming back if he goes ten thousand miles.
Oh, it's daddy'll tie my shoes,
And mommy'll glove my hands,
And you will kiss my ruby lips when you come back!
Look away, look away over Yandro.

I'll Give My Love An Apple

I'll ___ give my love an ap – ple with out – e'er a core. I'll ___
give my love a dwell – ing with out ___ e'er a door, I'll ____
give my love a pal – ace where – in she ___ might ___ be, That ____
she might un – lock it with – out e'er ___ a key.

How can there be an apple without e'er a core?
How can there be a dwelling without e'er a door?
How can there be a palace wherein she might be,
That she might unlock it without e'er a key?

My head is the apple without e'er a core,
My mind is the dwelling without e'er a door.
My heart is the palace wherein she might be,
That she might unlock it without e'er a key.

The Water Is Wide

A ship there is and she sails the sea,
She's loaded deep as deep can be.
But not so deep as the love I'm in,
And I know not how to sink or swim.

I leaned my back against a young oak,
Thinking he was a trusty tree.
But first he bended and then he broke,
And thus did my false love to me.

I put my hand into some soft bush,
Thinking the sweetest flower to find.
The thorn, it stuck me to the bone,
And, oh, I left that flower alone.

Oh, love is handsome and love is fine,
Gay as a jewel when first it's new.
But love grows old and waxes cold,
And fades away like summer dew.

Who's Gonna Shoe Your Pretty Little Foot?

Who's gon-na shoe your pret-ty lit-tle foot?

Who's gon-na glove ___ your hand? ___

Who's gon-na kiss ___ your red ru-by lips?

Who's gon-na be your man? ___

Who's gonna be your man?,
Who's gonna be your man?,
Who's gonna kiss your red ruby lips?,
Who's gonna be your man?

Well, papa's gonna shoe my pretty little foot,
Mama's gonna glove my hand,
And sister's gonna kiss my red ruby lips,
I don't need no man.

I don't need no man,
I don't need no man,
Sister's gonna kiss my red ruby lips,
I don't need no man.

The longest train I ever did see
Was a hundred coaches long,
The only woman I ever did love
Was on that train and gone.

On that train and gone,
On that train and gone,
The only woman I ever did love
Was on that train and gone.

21

Black Is The Color

I go to the river for to mourn and weep,
But satisfied I never can sleep,
I'll write to you in a few short lines,
I'll suffer death ten thousand times.

I know my love and well she knows,
I love the grass whereon she goes,
If she on earth no more I see,
My life will quickly fade away.

A winter's past and the leaves are green,
The time has passed that we have seen,
But still I hope the time will come,
When you and I will be as one.

The Queen of Hearts

I have a store on yonder mountain,
Where gold and silver are had for countin',
I cannot count for thought of thee,
My eyes so full I cannot see.

I love my father, I love my mother,
I love my sister, I love my brother,
I love my friends and relations too,
But I'd leave them all to go with you.

My father left me both house and land,
And servants many at my command,
At my command they ne'er shall be,
I'll leave them all to go with thee.

Pretty Saro

Down in some lone val - ley in a lone - some place, Where the
wild birds do whis - tle and their notes do in - crease, Fare -
well,____ pret - ty Sa - ro, I____ bid you a - dieu; And I'll
dream of pret - ty Sa - ro wher - ev - er I go.

My love she won't have me so I understand.
She wants a freeholder who owns house and land.
I cannot maintain her with silver and gold.
And all of the fine things a big house can hold.

If I were a merchant and could write a fine hand,
I'd write my love a letter that she'd understand.
I'd write her by the river, where the waters o'erflow.
But I'll dream of pretty Saro wherever I go.

Pretty Peggy-o

Come go along with me, Pretty Peggy-o,
Come go along with me, Pretty Peggy-o,
In coaches you shall ride with your true love by your side,
Just as grand as any lady in the are-o.

What would your mother think, Pretty Peggy-o?
What would your mother think, Pretty Peggy-o?
What would your mother think, for to hear the guineas clink,
And the soldiers all a-marching before ye-o?

You're the man that I adore, Handsome Willie-o,
You're the man that I adore, Handsome Willie-o,
You're the man that I adore but your fortune is too low,
I'm afraid my mother would be angry-o.

Come a-tripping down the stair, Pretty Peggy-o,
Come a-tripping down the stair, Pretty Peggy-o,
Come a-tripping down the stair and tie up your yellow hair,
Bid a last farewell to Handsome Willie-o.

If ever I return, Pretty Peggy-o,
If ever I return, Pretty Peggy-o,
If ever I return, the city I will burn,
And destroy all the ladies in the are-o.

Our captain, he is dead, Pretty Peggy-o,
Our captain, he is dead, Pretty Peggy-o,
Our captain, he is dead - and he died for a maid,
And he's buried in the Louisiana country-o.

Once I Had A Sweetheart

Once I had a sweet-heart and now I have none. Once I had a sweet-heart and now I have none. He's gone and leave me, he's gone and leave me, He's gone and leave me in sor-row to mourn.

One night in sweet sorrow I lay down to sleep *(2)*
My own fairest jewel, my own fairest jewel,
My own fairest jewel sat smiling at me.

My sweetheart is married or otherwise dead, *(2)*
His bunch of blue ribbons, his bunch of blue ribbons,
His bunch of blue ribbons, I'll wear 'round my head.

But when I awakend I found it not so, *(2)*
My eyes like some fountains, my eyes like some fountains,
My eyes like some fountains with tears overflow.

I'll travel through England, through France and through Spain, *(2)*
My life I will venture, my life I will venture,
My life I will venture on the watery main.

The Lily of The West

When first I came to Lou - is - ville, some plea - sure there to find, A
dam - sel there from Lex - ing - ton was plea - sing to my mind, Her
ros - y cheeks, her ru - by lips, like ar - rows pierced my breast, And the
name she bore was Flo - ra, _____ the Lil - y of the West.

I courted lovely Flora some pleasure there to find,
But she turned unto another man which sore distressed my mind.
She robbed me of my liberty, deprived me of my rest,
Then go my love Flora, the Lily of the West.

Way down in yonder shady grove, a man of high degree,
Conversing with my Flora there, it seemed so strange to me.
And the answer that she gave to him, it sore did me oppress,
I was betrayed by Flora, the Lily of the West.

I stepped up to my rival, my dagger in my hand,
I seized him by the collar and I boldly bade him stand.
Being mad to desperation I pierced him in the breast,
Then go my lovely Flora, the Lily of the West.

I had to stand my trial, I had to make my plea,
They placed me in a criminal box and then commenced on me.
Although she swore my life away, deprived my of my rest,
Still I love my faithless Flora, the Lily of the West.

Oh, My Little Darling

Oh, my lit - tle dar - ling, don't _____ you weep and cry,

some sweet day a - com - ing, mar - ry you and I

Oh, my little darling, don't you weep and moan,
Some sweet day coming, take my baby home.

Up and down the railroad, 'cross the county line,
Pretty little girl is funny, wife is always crying.

Oh, my little darling, don't you weep and cry,
Some sweet day a-coming, marry you and I.

The Turtle Dove

Poor lit-tle tur-tle dove, Set-ting on a pine, Long-ing for his own true love, As I did once for mine, for mine, As I did once for mine.

I come down the mountainside
I give my horn a blow
Everywhere them pretty girls
Said yonder goes my beau, my beau,
Yonder goes my beau.

I walked down the street that very same night,
On my heart was a sweet, sweet song
Got in a fight and in jail all night
And every durn thing went wrong, went wrong,
Every durn thing went wrong.

I went down in the valley green
To win to me my love,
When I done with that pretty little girl
She turned to a turtle dove, a dove,
She turned to a turtle dove.

I went up on the mountainside
And took a swig of corn
Possum wrapped his tail around a blackberry bush
Two mountain lions were born, were born,
Two mountain lions were born.

Must I Go Bound

I put my finger to the bush,
To pluck a rose of fairest kind.
The thorn, it pierced me at the touch,
And oh, I left the rose behind.

Must I go bound while you go free?
Must I love a lad that don't love me?
Was e'er I taught to play the part,
To love the lad who'd break my heart?

Love is Pleasing

I left my mother, I left my father,
I left my brother and my sisters, too.
I left my home and kind relations,
I left them all for the love of you.

If I'd a-known before I courted,
That love had a-been such a killin' crime,
I'd a-locked my heart in a box of golden,
And tied it up with a silver twine.

I'm Sad and I'm Lonely

I'm sad and I'm lone-ly, my heart it will break. _ My

true love loves an-oth-er, Lord, I wish I was dead. _

Young ladies take warning,
Take warning from me,
Don't waste your affections
On a young man so free.

My cheeks once were red
Like the red, red rose;
But now they are white
As the lily that grows.

He'll hug you and he'll kiss you
And he'll tell you more lies
Than the cross-ties on the railroad
Or the stars in the sky.

I'll build me a cabin
On the mountain so high,
Where the blackbirds can't find me
Or hear my sad cry.

I'm troubled, yes, I'm troubled,
I'm troubled in my mind,
If this trouble don't kill me,
I'll live a long time.

If I Had Wings

If I had wings like No-ah's dove, _____ I'd fly up the riv-er_____ to the man I

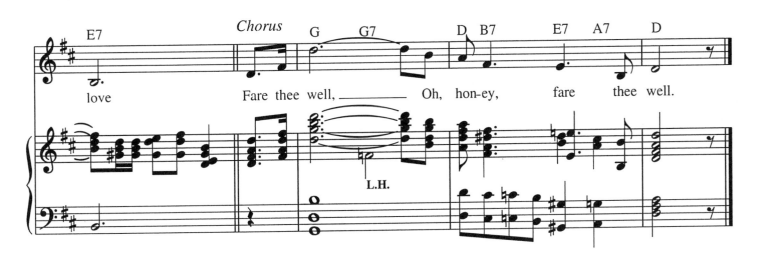

love Fare thee well, _____ Oh, hon-ey, fare thee well.

I've got a man and he's long and tall,
Moves his body like a cannon ball. *Chorus*

One of these days, and it won't be long,
Call my name and I'll be gone. *Chorus*

'Member one night, a-drizzlin' rain,
Round my heart I felt a pain. *Chorus*

When I wore my apron low,
Couldn't keep you from my door. *Chorus*

Now I wear my apron high,
Scarcely ever see you passin' by. *Chorus*

Now my apron's up to my chin,
You pass my door and you won't come in. *Chorus*

If I had listened to what my mama said,
I'd be at home in my mama's bed. *Chorus*

Go Way From My Window

I'll give you back your presents,
I'll give you back your ring;
But I won't forget my own true love,
As long as songbirds sing. (2)

I'll tell all of my brothers,
I'll tell my sisters, too;
The reason that my heart is broke,
Is all because of you. (2)

Go 'way in the springtime,
Come back in the fall;
Bring us back more money,
Than the both of us can haul. (2)

40

Jeanie With The Light Brown Hair

Words and Music by
Stephen C. Foster

dream of Jean-ie with the light brown _ hair, Float-ing like a va-por on the

soft sum-mer air.

I long for Jeanie with the day-dawn smile,
Radiating gladness warm with winning guile.
I hear her melodies, like joy gone by,
Sighing 'round my heart o'er the fond hopes that die.
Sighing like the night wind, sobbing like the rain,
Waiting for the lost one that comes not again.
I long for Jeanie and my heart bows low,
Never more to find her where the bright waters flow.

I sigh for Jeanie, but her light form strayed,
Far from the fond hearts 'round her native glade.
Her smiles have vanished and her sweet songs flown,
Flitting like the dreams that have cheered us and gone.
Now the nodding wild flow'rs may wither on the shore,
While her gentle fingers will cull them no more.
I sigh for Jeanie with the light brown hair,
Floating like a vapor on the soft summer air.

Ellen Bayne

Words and Music by
Stephen C. Foster

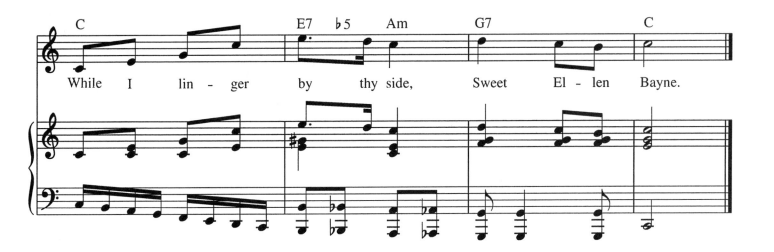

While I lin-ger by thy side, Sweet El-len Bayne.

Dream not in anguish,
Dream not in fear;
Love shall not languish,
Fond ones are near.
Sleeping or waking,
In pleasure or pain,
Warm hearts will beat for thee,
Sweet Ellen Bayne. *Chorus*

Scenes that have vanished
Smile on thee now.
Pleasures once banished,
Play 'round thy brow.
Forms long departed
Greet thee again,
Soothing thy dreaming heart,
Sweet Ellen Bayne. *Chorus*

Come Where My Love Lies Dreaming

Words and Music by
Stephen C. Foster

Come where my love lies dream - ing, Dream-ing the hap-py hours a - way, In

vis-ions bright re - deem - ing, The fleet-ing joys of day;

Dream - ing the hap-py hours, Dream-ing the hap-py hours a - way;

Come where my love lies dream - ing, Is sweet-ly dream- ing the hap-py hours a - way. ____

Come where my love lies dream - ing, Is sweet-ly dream-ing, her beau-ty beam - ing;

Come where my love lies dream - ing, Is sweet-ly dream- ing the hap-py hours a - way. ____

Come with the lute, Come with the lay, My own love is sweet-ly dream-ing, her beau-ty beam- ing.

Come where my love lies dream-ing, Is sweet-ly dream-ing the hap-py hours a - way.

Interlude

Soft is her slum-ber. Thoughts bright and free Dance through her dreams, like gush-ing mel-o-dy;

Light is her young heart, Light may it be! Come where my love lies dream - ing,

Dream - ing the hap-py hours, Dream-ing the hap-py hours a - way;

48

Gentle Annie

Words and Music by
Stephen C. Foster

Thou wilt come no more, gen- tle An- nie, Like a
We have roamed and loved 'mid the bow- ers, When thy
Ah! the hours grow sad while I pon- der, Near the

flow'r, thy spir- it did de - part; Thou art gone, a - las! like the
down - y cheeks were in their bloom; Now I stand a - lone 'mid the
si - lent spot where thou art laid, And my heart bows down when I

man - y That have bloomed in the sum- mer of my heart.
flow- ers, While they min - gle their per- fumes o'er thy tomb.
wan - der. By the stream and the mead- ows where we strayed.

Beautiful Dreamer

Words and Music by
Stephen C. Foster

Beautiful dreamer, out on the sea
Mermaids are chanting the wild Lorelei,
Over the streamlet vapors are borne
Waiting to fade at the bright coming morn.
Beautiful dreamer, beam on my heart
E'en as the morn on the streamlet and sea,
Then will all clouds of sorrow depart.
Beautiful dreamer, awake unto me.
Beautiful dreamer, awake unto me.

Somebody's Coming To See Me Tonight

Words and Music by
Stephen C. Foster

Somebody's coming to see me tonight,
Somebody's presence is dear to my sight.
Somebody's cheeks are as red as the rose,
Somebody's sorry when somebody goes. *Chorus*

Somebody often times gives me a kiss,
Somebody'll meet me enraptured with bliss.
Somebody says I'm the joy of his life,
And soon I'm to be that somebody's wife. *Chorus*

Jenny June

Words by George Cooper

Music by Stephen C. Foster

Did you see dear Jen - ny June When the mead - ows were in tune with the

birds a - mong the bow - ers in the sweet sum - mer time. You would

love her, I am sure, For her heart is warm and pure And as

guile - less as the flow - ers in the sweet sum - mer time.

All the robins cease their song
As she gaily speeds along,
Just to listen to her singing
In the sweet summer time.
And her modest beaming eyes
Are the color of the skies;
Many pleasant fancies bringing
In the sweet summer time. *Chorus*

With my darling Jenny June,
When the meadows are in tune,
Just to listen to her singing
In the sweet summer time,
While her presence seems to be
Like a ray of light to me,
For she's ever fond and loving
In the sweet summer time.   *Chorus*

Wait For The Wagon

Words and Music by
R. Bishop Buckley *c.*1850

Where the river runs like silver, and birds they sing so sweet,
I have a cabin, Phillis, and something good to eat.
Come listen to my story, it will relieve my heart,
So jump into the wagon, and off we will start. *Chorus*

Do you believe, my Phillis, dear, old Mike with all his wealth,
Can make you half so happy, as I with youth and health?
We'll have a little farm, a horse, a pig and cow;
And you will mind the dairy, while I guide the plough. *Chorus*

Your lips are red as poppies, your hair so slick and neat,
All braided up with dahlias, and hollyhocks so sweet.
It's ev'ry Sunday morning, when I am by your side,
We'll jump into the wagon, and all take a ride. *Chorus*

Together on life's journey, we'll travel till we stop,
And if we have no trouble, we'll reach the happy top.
Then come with me, sweet Phillis, my dear, my lovely bride,
We'll jump into the wagon, and all take a ride. *Chorus*

Seeing Nellie Home

Words by
Francis Kyle

Music by
James Fletcher
c. 1840

In the sky the bright stars glit- tered, _____ On the bank the pale moon shone. It was from Aunt Di - nah's quilt-ing par-ty I was, see - ing Nel-lie home. I was see - ing Nel-lie home, _____ I was see - ing Nel-lie home. It was

Chorus

from Aunt Di – nah's quilt-ing par-ty I was see – ing Nel - lie home.

On my arm soft hand rested,
Rested light as ocean foam.
It was from Aunt Dinah's quilting party,
I was seeing Nellie home. *Chorus*

On my lips a whisper trembled,
Trembled till it dared to come.
It was from Aunt Dinah's quilting party,
I was seeing Nellie home. *Chorus*

On my life new hopes were dawning,
And those hopes have lived and grown.
It was from Aunt Dinah's quilting party,
I was seeing Nellie home. *Chorus*

Aura Lee

Words by W. W. Fosdick

Music by George R. Poulton
1861

As the black-bird in the spring, 'Neath the wil - low tree

Sat and piped, I heard him sing, Sing of Au - ra Lee.

Au - ra Lee, Au - ra Lee, Maid of gold - en hair,

Sun - shine came a - long with thee, And swal - lows in the air.

In thy blush the rose was born;
Music when you spake.
Through thine azure eyes the moon
Sparkling seemed to break.
Aura Lee, Aura Lee,
Birds of crimson wing
Never song have sung to me
As in that bright, sweet spring.

Aura Lee, the bird may flee,
The willow's golden hair
Swing through winter fitfully,
On the stormy air.
Yet if thy blue eyes I see,
Gloom will soon depart.
For to me, sweet Aura Lee
Is sunshine through the heart.

When the mistletoe was green,
'Midst the winter's snows,
Sunshine in thy face was seen.
Kissing lips of rose,
Aura Lee, Aura Lee,
Take my golden ring.
Love and light return with thee,
And swallows with the spring.

She's The Sweetest Of Them All

Will S. Hays
1869

O! I have met a charm-er, She's sweet to gaze up - on. The first time that you see her face, You feel your heart is gone, She wears her dress *"au pan - ier,"* She's nei-ther short nor tall, And of all the charm-ing girls in town, She's the sweet-est of them all.

She plays upon the piano,
The jaw's harp and bazoon,
And when she hasn't got a cold,
Sing "Up In A Balloon."
She goes to balls and parties,
And when her name they call,
The men all look around to see
The sweetest of them all. *Chorus*

I asked her if she'd have me,
She smiled and said, "You bet."
Then whispered sweetly in my ear,
"We may be happy yet."
There's going to be a wedding
Some time late in the fall,
And I'm to be the better half
Of the sweetest of them all. *Chorus*

I'm going to build a mansion
With a big plate on the door,
And put my name upon it:
"A. Junius Brutus Moore."
I'm going to give a party,
And invite you folks to call,
And see how happy I will be
With the sweetest of them all. *Chorus*

65

Juanita

Words and Music by
Caroline Norton *c.* 1890

Soft o'er the foun - tain, ling -'ring falls the south-ern moon,

Far o'er the moun - tain, breaks the day too soon.

In thy dark eye's splen - dor, where the warm light loves to dwell,

Wear - y looks, yet ten – der, speak the fond fare – well.

When in thy dreaming moons like these shall shine again,
And daylight beaming, prove thy dreams are vain;
Wilt thou not relenting, for thine absent lover sigh?
In thy hear consenting to a prayer gone by?
Nita! Juanita! Let me linger by thy side!
Nita! Juanita! Be may own fair bride.

O Cupid, Sweet Cupid

A. Nelson Adams
1894

He: O Cu - pid, Sweet Cu - pid, Come hith - er I pray, Thy gra - ces I

fain would em - ploy._____ Make haste, for my peace is well

nigh gone a - stray, Then be not so tim - id and coy,_____ Your

of - fice of rap - ture, Your joy and de - light, In quick re - qui -

She: O Cupid, sweet Cupid, why seekest thou me,
Nor enter without an alarm?
'Tis mischief that brings thee, I plainly can see,
I pray thee, then do me no harm.
　　Sweet cherub, thine arrows have pierced to my heart,
　　Thou tyrant, Why givest me pain?
　　Yet stay, I'll not chide thee nor pluck one wee dart,
　　Though they pierce and repierce me again.

Chorus (Both)

　　Ah! then Cupid, sweet Cupid, why seekest thou me,
　　Now leave me alone with the past.
　　Thy mischief is done and I plainly can see,
　　Thou, sweet tyrant, has conquered at last.

Both: O Cupid, sweet Cupid, thy mission is done,
Thine arts thou didst nobly employ.
Two hearts thou hast joined and cemented in one,
And seeded with rapture and joy.
　　Henceforth I beseech thee, abide thou in peace,
　　Nor wander from hearts thou hast won.
　　Thine office, sweet Cupid, I pray thee ne'er cease,
　　Like your mission, 'tis but just begun.

Chorus (Both)

　　Ah! then, Cupid, sweet Cupid, bide thou in peace,
　　Nor wander from hearts thou hast won.
　　Thine office, sweet Cupid, I pray thee ne'er cease,
　　Like your mission, 'tis but just begun.

I'll Remember You In My Prayers

Will S. Hays
1869

And at night when I kneel by my bed-side and pray, I'll re-
mem - ber you love, in my prayers.

I have loved you too fondly to ever forget
The love you have spoken for me,
And the kiss of affection still warm on my lips,
When you told me how true you would be.
    I know not if Fortune be fickle or friend,
    Or if time on your memory wears;
    I know that I love wherever you roam,
    And remember you, love, in my prayers. *Chorus*

When heavenly angels are guarding the good,
As God has ordained them to do,
In answer to prayers I have offered to Him,
I know there is one watching you.
    And may its bright spirit be with you through life,
    To guide you up heaven's bright stairs,
    And meet with the one who has loved you so true,
    And remembered you, love, in her prayers. *Chorus*

The Sweetest Story Ever Told

Words and Music by
R. M. Stults *c.*1880

I Took Her To The Ball

Will S. Hays
1877

One af-ter-noon in sum-mer. I met her on Broad-way, We smiled up-on each

oth-er, And met a-gain next day. She told me that she loved me, And

said that I must call, And on that ver-y eve-ning I took her to the ball. O!

Chorus

She was fair and love-ly, The queen a-mong them

all._____ She would not dance with none but me, For I took___ her__ to the ball,_____ Her ____

Dance

Fine

Her cheeks were like two roses,
Her teeth were pearly white,
Her eyes were bright as diamonds,
And glistened in the night.
    Her voice was like sweet music,
    O! take her all in all,
    She looked just like an angel,
    I took her to the ball. *Chorus*

And when we were returning,
I asked her on the way,
If she would like to marry -
If so, to name the day.
So we are to be married,
Quite early in the fall.
The way I came to get her-
I took her to the ball. *Chorus*

The Danza

Words and Music by
George Whitefield Chadwick
1885

Composer's original arrangement transposed from F.

If you
nev - er have danced The Dan - za, With its
won - drous rhyth- mic twirl, While close to your
bo - som pant- ed, Some dark - eyed

By I - nez I was taught,

In the gar - den splashed the foun tain,

Where the palm trees hid the

May I Print A Kiss

Words and Music by
Carrie Jacobs Bond
c. 1910

"May I print a kiss on your lips!" he said, She nod - ded her kind per - mis - sion. They went to press, And I rath - er guess, They print-ed a whole___ e - di - tion, They print-ed a whole___ e - di - tion.

Waltz

Words and Music by
Charles Ives
1895

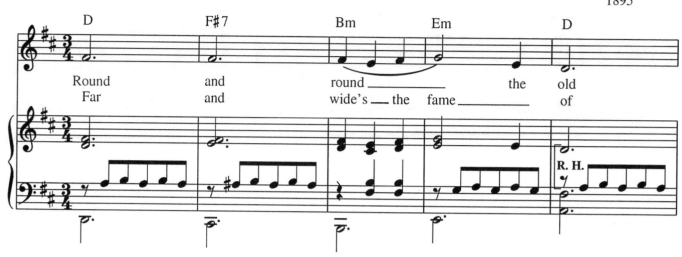

Round   and   round ____ the old
Far   and   wide's __ the fame ____ of

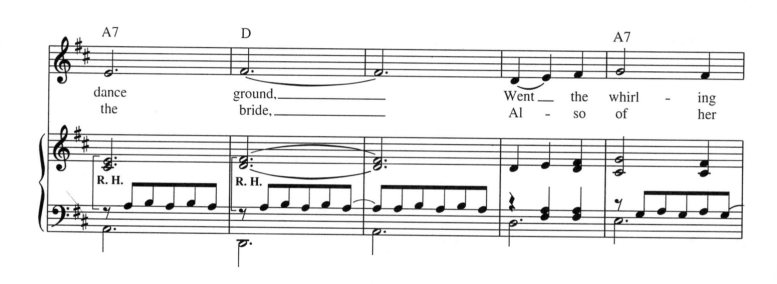

dance   ground, ____ Went __ the whirl - ing
the   bride, ____ Al - so of her

throng, ____ Moved _ with wine   and   song;
beau, ____ Ev -'ry - one knows   it's "Joe.

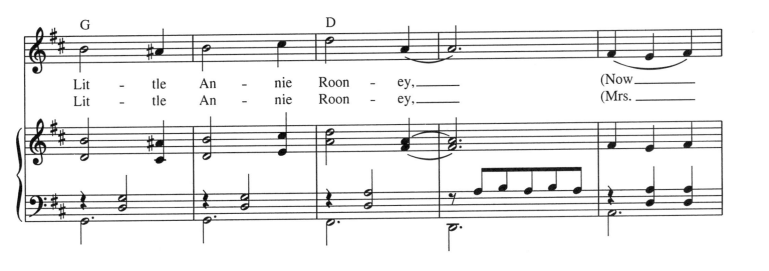

Will You Love Me In December

As You Do In May?

Words by
James J. Walker

Music by
Ernest R. Ball
1905

Now in the sum - mer of life sweet-heart, You say you love but
You say the glow on my cheek, sweet-heart, Is like the rose so

me, Glad - ly I give all my heart to you,
sweet; But when the bloom of fair youth has flown,

When You Were Sweet Sixteen

Words and Music by
James Thornton
1898

Chorus

I love you as I nev-er lov'd be-fore,___ Since first I met you on the vil - lage

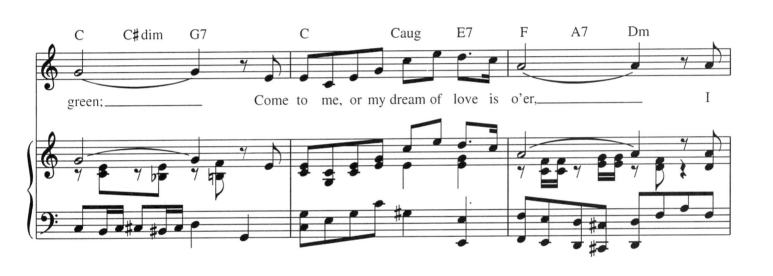

green;___ Come to me, or my dream of love is o'er,___ I

love you as I lov'd you when you were sweet, When you were sweet six-teen.

My Blushing Rosie

Words by Edgar Smith

Music by John Stromberg
1900

There's a charm-ing bud of beau-ty that I long to call my
talk a-bout your dai-sies, And the sweet for-get - me-

bride, And I'm real-ly nev-er hap-py less my ba-by's by my
not; But the sim-ple lit-tle rose-bud sets me cra-zy on the

side. Her bap-tis-mal name is Ro-sie, But she puts the rose to
spot. There is man-y a gaud-y flow-er with a fine high sound - ing

shame; And most an-y night you'll hear me call her name.
name, But my rose is in my bow-er just the same.

Can't You Hear Me Callin', Caroline

Words by
WM. H. Gardner

Music by
Caro Roma
1914

line,   Car - o - line;   I   miss you when the moon-beams   out
line,   Car - o - line;   I   miss your hand a - steal - in'   so

on the riv -er shine,   Oh,   can't you hear me call - in'   for you, Car - o-line.
trust - in' like in   mine,   Oh,   can't you hear me call - in'   for you, Car - o-line.

rit.

Can't   you hear me   call-in', Car-o-line,   It's my heart a- call - in'   thine.

a tempo

98

Lordy, how I miss you, gal o' mine, Wish that I could kiss you Car-o-

line! Ain't no use now for the sun to shine, Car-o-

line, Car-o-line, Can't you hear my lips a-say-in',

Can't you hear my soul a-pray-in', Can't you hear me call-in', Car-o-line.

There's A Long, Long Trail

Stoddard King

Zo Elliott
1914

Nights are grow – ing ver – y lone – ly, Days are ver – y
All night long I hear you call – ing, Call – ing sweet and

long; _____ I'm a – grow – ing wear – y on – – ly
low; _____ Seem to hear your foot – steps fall – – ing,

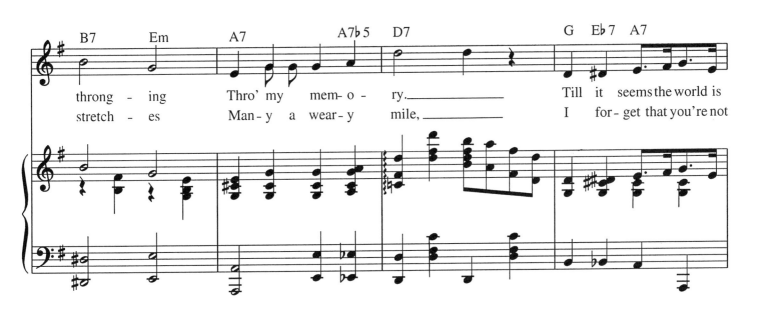

My Melancholy Baby

The Sweetheart Of Sigma Chi

Words by
Byron D. Stokes

Music by F. Dudleigh Vernor
1912

sky; _____ And the moon - light beams on the girl of my

dreams, She's the Sweet - heart of Sig - ma Chi. _____

Let Me Call You Sweetheart

Words by
Beth Slater Whitson

Music by
Leo Friedman
1910

For Me And My Gal

Words and Music by
Edgar Leslie, E. Ray Goetz and George Meyer
1917